Dear Parents and Teachers,

Reading chapter books is a very exciting step in your child's life as a reader.

With Hello Reader Chapter Books, our goal is to bring the excitement of chapter books together with appropriate content and vocabulary so that children take pride in their success as readers.

Children like to read independently, but you can share this experience with them to make it even more rewarding. Here are some tips to try:

- Read the book aloud for the first time.
- Point out the chapter headings.
- Look at the illustrations. Can your child find words in the text that match the pictures?
- After you or your child finishes reading a chapter, ask what might happen in the next chapter.
- Praise your child throughout the reading of the book.
- And if your child wants to read alone, then take out your own book or magazine and read sitting side by side!

Remember, reading is a joy to share. So, have fun experiencing your child's new ability to read chapter books!

Francie Alexander
Vice President and Chief Academic Officer
Scholastic Education

D0062669

*For Olivia, who would love to meet
a talking snowman! XOXO!*
— Mommy

*For William, Sarah, and Christopher,
master snowman makers!*
— D.S.

ISBN 0-439-57744-6

Text copyright © 2004 by Kathryn Cristaldi.
Illustrations copyright © 2004 by David Sheldon.
All rights reserved. Published by Scholastic Inc.

SCHOLASTIC, HELLO READER, and
associated logos are trademarks and/or
registered trademarks of Scholastic Inc.

12 11 10 9 8 7   6 7 8 9/0

Printed in the U.S.A.
First printing, February 2004

THE SNOWMAN MYSTERY

by Kathryn Cristaldi
Illustrated by David Sheldon

SCHOLASTIC INC.
New York   Toronto   London   Auckland   Sydney
Mexico City   New Delhi   Hong Kong   Buenos Aires

CHAPTER 1

Max and Miles were best friends.
They did everything together.

They rode their bikes in the park.

They played catch.

They raked leaves.

They played games on the computer.

One day it snowed.
Max called Miles.

"Let's build a snowman," he said.
"Tomorrow!" said Miles.
"It will be our best snowman ever!"
said Max.

CHAPTER 2

Max and Miles walked to school
the next day.

There was a new boy at school.
His name was Brad.
Brad was bad.

He put gum on Max's chair.

He pushed Miles on the playground.
Max and Miles did not like Brad.

Miles went to Max's house after
school.
They built a snowman.

Then they saw Brad.
"Uh-oh," said Max.
"This snowman stinks," said Brad.

Max wanted to scare Brad.
"Don't get our snowman mad,"
said Max.
"He's alive and he's mean!"

Brad just laughed.

CHAPTER 3

Max and Miles had a plan.
They were going to get even
with bad Brad.

They were going to really
scare him.

Miles and Max got a tape recorder.
They turned it on.

They made scary noises.

Max and Miles took the tape
recorder outside.

They hid behind the snowman.
They waited and waited.

Brad came down the block.

Miles turned on the tape recorder.
"WAAAA!" screamed the snowman.

"He's alive!" Brad cried.
He ran and hid behind a tree.

Max and Miles laughed so hard.
They fell on the ground.

Brad saw Max and Miles.
Then Brad began to laugh.

"That was funny," he said.
"I never met a talking snowman."

"He just moved here," said Max.
Then they all began to laugh.